*For Leovander, who is nearly always
full of the joys of spring!
~ S S*

*For Kathryn, my dancing, surfing,
singing partner in crime, and fellow foodie!
~ C P*

LITTLE TIGER PRESS LTD,
an imprint of the Little Tiger Group
1 Coda Studios, 189 Munster Road, London SW6 6AW
www.littletiger.co.uk

First published in Great Britain 2020
This edition published 2021

Text copyright © Steve Smallman 2020
Illustrations copyright © Caroline Pedler 2020
Steve Smallman and Caroline Pedler have asserted their rights to be identified as the author
and illustrator of this work under the Copyright, Designs and Patents Act, 1988

A CIP catalogue record for this book is available from the British Library

Printed in China • LTP/1400/2933/0919

2 4 6 8 10 9 7 5 3 1

A Friend for Bear

Steve Smallman   Caroline Pedler

LITTLE TIGER

LONDON

All through the long, cold winter,
Little Bear had slept safe and
snug in her den.

Then, at last, a warm breeze
melted away the forest frost.
Little Bear's eyes blinked open,
and she bounced out of bed!

"IT'S SPRING!" she cried, racing outside.
Everything was fresh, and green, and sparkly.
Little Bear felt dizzy with the joy of it all!
"I WANT TO RUN AND JUMP AND SMELL
FLOWERS AND TICKLE TADPOLES!"
she shouted.

"And I mustn't forget TWIRLING!"
She twirled round so fast . . .

she tripped over a stone!
But it wasn't a stone.

It was a tortoise.

"Whoops-a-daisy!" said Tortoise.
"Are you all right?"

"I was just twirling!" said Little Bear.
"Because IT'S SPRIIIIIIIIIIIIIIIING! Next I'm
going to do roly-polying, climbing trees,
and making new friends."

"That sounds wonderful," beamed Tortoise.
"Come with me!" suggested Little Bear.
"Oh, I couldn't keep up," sighed Tortoise.
"I've only got plodding legs."
"That's OK," laughed Little Bear, lifting
Tortoise up. "I'll give you a piggyback."
And off they went!

"Goodness!" laughed Tortoise. "I've never moved so fast!"

"Can we play?" called two fox cubs.

But Little Bear galloped right past them.

"Little Bear," cried Tortoise, "I thought making new friends was on your list?"

"It is!" replied Little Bear. "But I haven't finished running yet!"

They burst into a meadow peppered with primroses.
  "Can't we stop and smell the flowers?" pleaded Tortoise.
  "No time to stop — too much to do!" laughed
Little Bear. "Start smelling!"
  "Ouch!" grumbled Tortoise, as a bumblebee bounced
off his head. "My nose won't work at this speed!"
  But Little Bear was running too fast to hear him.

Little Bear finally skidded to a halt
at the top of a small hill.
Tortoise looked around in wonder.
"I've never been so high!" he gasped.
"I can see the world! Thank you,
Little Bear, this is perfect."

"PERFECT FOR ROLY-POLYING!" finished
Little Bear. And clutching Tortoise tightly,
she rolled over and over, all the way
down the hill.

They stopped with a bump at the foot of a tall tree.

"Time to climb!" declared Little Bear.

"Oh, no," groaned Tortoise, his head spinning. "Can't I just sit—"

"—ON MY SHOULDERS? GOOD IDEA!" finished Little Bear. And up they went!

Mummy Bird was very surprised!
"Shoo!" she flapped.
"Time to go!" whispered Tortoise.
"TIME TO TICKLE TADPOLES!"
bellowed Little Bear. "TO THE POND!"

"What a day!" puffed Tortoise, as he flopped down by the water's edge. Little Bear dropped down beside him.
They watched ducklings and tadpoles playing in the water.
"Are you thinking what I'm thinking?" asked Little Bear.
"Yes," sighed Tortoise dreamily, "this is a lovely spot . . ."

"... TO JUMP FROM!" cheered Little Bear.
Then she grabbed Tortoise and leapt into the pond!

"Wasn't that great?" laughed Little Bear, scrambling out.
But Tortoise had had enough. "NO!" he spluttered.
"I CAN'T SWIM! MY SHELL IS FULL OF WATER AND
THERE'S PONDWEED IN MY PANTS!"
"But you wanted to swim!" said Little Bear in surprise.
"NO I DID NOT!" snorted Tortoise.

"You never stop to listen, or think, or make friends!" he finished.

"But there's SO much to do!" cried Little Bear. "I can't stop!"

"Well, you'll have to," declared Tortoise, "because it's bedtime!"

"NOOOOOOOOOOO!" howled Little Bear. "I'M NOT TIRED! I DON'T WANT TO GO BACK TO BED FOR EVER AND EVER! I WANT IT TO BE SPRING AGAIN!"

"Oh, Little Bear," smiled Tortoise,
"it's not time to hibernate yet!
Tomorrow will still be spring."
"It will?" sniffled Little Bear.
"And can I do running and
twirling and climbing?"

"Yes!" nodded Tortoise. "And maybe some
sitting and watching too!"

"Do you think I might find some
friends?" Little Bear whispered.

"I'm sure you will!" chuckled Tortoise.
"You've already found one today!"

"Have I?" asked Little Bear. "Who?"

"Me, Little Bear," said Tortoise. "Me."

Little Bear beamed. "Shall I give you a ride back home? We can go slowly if you like."

"Let's go fast instead!" suggested Tortoise with a grin.

So Little Bear lifted him up onto her back and they zoomed off together, all the way home to bed.

More warm and wonderful stories to share from Little Tiger Press...

Scaredy BEAR
Steve Smallman
Caroline Pedler

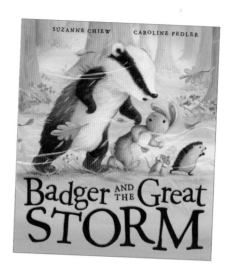

Badger AND THE Great STORM
SUZANNE CHIEW · CAROLINE PEDLER

Tiger Tiger
Jonny Lambert

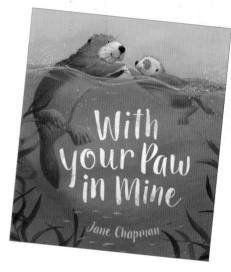

With your Paw in Mine
Jane Chapman

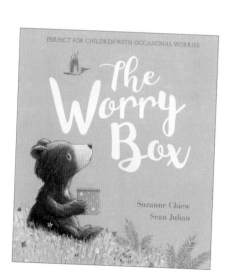

PERFECT FOR CHILDREN WITH OCCASIONAL WORRIES

The Worry Box
Suzanne Chiew
Sean Julian

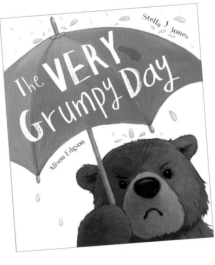

Stella J Jones

The VERY Grumpy Day
Alison Edgson

For information regarding any of the above titles
or for our catalogue, please contact us:
Little Tiger Press Ltd, 1 Coda Studios,
189 Munster Road, London SW6 6AW
Tel: 020 7385 6333
E-mail: contact@littletiger.co.uk
www.littletiger.co.uk